A LOVE SONG TO CHERISH

JOSIE RIVIERA

READER REVIEWS

"Riviera weaves wondrous tales of love, betrayal, and forgiveness."

"How awesome is this author. She has her pulse on her readers."

"Josie Riviera's writing evokes tender emotions and a deep understanding of God's love for us and our love for others. All of her books are a must-read for those who appreciate genuine love from a Christian perspective. Thank you Josie Riviera!"

"I was feeling down and this book gave me a happy sigh."

"Another Josie Riviera book that kept me up way too late!"

"Oh .... BUY BUY BUY BUY BUY!
    I sometimes get so tired of reading..... for all seems the same lately... THIS IS NOT THE SAME! I was so surprised that I was totally involved in the story from page one. I had a

very difficult time rejoining the real world long enough to cook and shower! I read all day... and late into the night. I hated the fact the story ended. I want more more more! I enjoyed every character, the plot, the way it is set up and the way the entire story starts, continues and ends. This author is not one of my normal ones .... However, after this... I will look for this author! So buy the book and most of all, make sure you have time to read it without a lot of interruptions."

"I loved this story. The research and details were great. I liked the ending. It was heartwarming. I cried a lot. I recommend everyone read this book."

INTRODUCTION

To keep up on newly released ebooks, paperbacks, Large Print Paperbacks, audiobooks, as well as exclusive sales, sign up for Josie's Newsletter today.

As a thank you, I'll send you a Free PDF ... The Beauty Of ...

Josie's Newsletter

Did you know that according to a Yale University study, people who read books live longer?

This book is dedicated to all my wonderful readers who have supported me every inch of the way.
THANK YOU!

PRAISE AND AWARDS

USA TODAY bestselling author
#1 Bestseller Women's Religious Fiction
#1 Bestseller Contemporary Religious Fiction
#1 Bestseller Inspirational Religious Fiction

CHAPTER ONE

*D*orothy Thompson had vowed to never set foot in Cherish, South Carolina again. She didn't want to come back here. She couldn't face it.

Sure, she'd lived in the tiny town all her life. And she'd felt alone, despite her popularity, her cheerleader friends, her football player boyfriend. Her mother had orchestrated Dorothy's status, keeping one eye on the stylish girls and the other eye on Dorothy.

"Everything will be perfect once you meet the right man, provided he's rich," her mother had explained. "A poor man does no more good than an eyeless needle."

Nonetheless, everything hadn't been perfect. Dorothy's wealthy boyfriend had cheated on her, and she couldn't compete with the stunning platinum blondes and redheads once she entered high school.

She'd told her mother she didn't care a cow-eatin' cabbage about who liked her and who didn't, although she knew it wasn't true. Her popularity had mattered very much during her tumultuous teens.

All this went through her mind while she parked her Ford

Escort rental in front of Memorial Street Church. She regarded the church's white-painted exterior, the high-arched windows with their beautiful stained glass depicting scenes from the Bible and the ornately carved heavy wooden doors. Memories whispered of her singing beloved hymns in the church choir and memorizing Bible verses in Sunday school in the church's basement.

So many memories for one little town.

She leaned her head against the driver's seat, no space in her mind for anything except sleep. The previous month, she'd endured the acute stage of opiate withdrawal along with the palpitations and tremors that came with it. And now Dr. Gantori, Dorothy's physician, had said the post-acute withdrawal stage could last two years.

She rubbed a hand over her puffy eyes. She was exhausted, and no wonder. With a sigh, she reached for the bag of chocolate chip cookies she'd purchased at the train station. The bag was surprisingly light. Had she mindlessly eaten the entire contents on the drive?

She rummaged in the bottom of the bag for one last cookie and chewed slowly, vowing to eat healthier tomorrow. The Cherish Hills Inn, the rental she'd booked for the week, boasted a kitchen, so there were no excuses. Besides, she was a good cook.

Dusting her fingers on a napkin in the glove compartment, she grabbed a bottled water and scooped up her leather briefcase stuffed with music.

Her palms were sweaty. She hesitated.

Fear of what might go wrong stopped her from getting out of the car. It had never occurred to her to let Dr. Gantori know she'd be traveling to another corner of the country. What would happen if she ran out of pain medication or experienced a panic attack and her hands froze to the piano keys?

Get back in the game. Keep God as the priority.

She lowered her car window and gazed outside, focusing on deep breaths in and out.

A fold of sleek silver clouds drifted across a robin's egg blue sky—a typical spring day in South Carolina. She knew the weather by heart. The air was mild, blowing a slight breeze against her cheeks. A hound dog lay basking on the sidewalk in the bright noonday sun.

Relax your muscles. Think positively.

She wiped her palms on her tweed skirt. There were pharmacies everywhere, she assured herself, and Dr. Gantori was merely a phone call away. Still, a knot threatened to take up residence in her stomach. What if the doctor didn't answer when she called?

Her brows puckered, her thoughts scattered. *No, no, no.* She bridled her panic. The task of chastising herself was growing thin as frustration poked through her anxiety. Undoubtedly, the doctor used a twenty-four-hour answering service.

She was back in Cherish for her brother, not herself. It was high time she rearranged her priorities. There was more to her story than failing to become a concert performer. Through her difficult year of wrist pain when she'd become angry with God, she'd wanted to run away from her problems, disengaging from friends, social media, and to be truthful, from life.

If only her carpal tunnel hadn't been so excruciating, if only she hadn't become addicted to pain relievers ...

If only ... If only ...

But she had, and she'd become an addict.

However, she'd come through the storm intact and had learned to keep her trust in God, because He had her name on something else. But she didn't know what. She only knew it wasn't a concert career.

"Everyone has doubts after a poor performance," Dorothy mumbled, lifting a brief prayer. "What matters is how we react to them."

Holding that thought, she drew her shoulders straight, grabbed her canvas quilted jacket, tasseled purse and briefcase, and stepped from the car.

Her gaze landed on the top step of Memorial Street Church and a rollicking laugh gave her pause.

"Dorothy Thompson, is that really you?" Marge Addyson, the church's associate pastor and the clergy person elected to officiate the wedding ceremony, greeted Dorothy with a flash of a smile that could pass for heat lightning. "Why, you're all grown up. I haven't seen you since your parents went to be with the Lord."

"It's been five years since their funerals." Dorothy gulped air as she replied, that familiar despondency stabbing her heart. Her parent's car accident should never have happened. Her father had always been careful when he drove, mindfully watching the speed limit, and only twenty miles outside of Cherish on the highway near St. Luke's hospital ... no one could have predicted a fatal accident where the other driver was strung-out on drugs.

"When did you arrive in Cherish?" Mrs. Addyson asked.

"Just now." Dorothy gazed heavenward, grateful for the change in subject. "I rented a car at the Cherish Central train station." Her proper black pumps echoed across the pavement as she made her way up the church steps. "Where's Pastor Steven and his wife, Christina?"

"They're taking a well-deserved vacation. You're sure to see them both when they return in two weeks."

She wouldn't be staying in Cherish for two weeks, Dorothy thought, although there was no need to share that information with the kind associate pastor.

When Dorothy reached the church's entryway, Mrs.

Addyson embraced her in a warm hug. "I'm happy as the bluebonnets blooming in spring that you could come back for Nicholas' wedding. I hope it wasn't difficult taking time away from your prominent concert engagements."

Prominent concert engagements? A distant memory. Paying the rent on her expensive apartment in New York City? Not so distant.

"No worries." Dorothy fingered the corners of her worn leather briefcase. "I'd never refuse my big brother anything, nor miss seeing him and Alice get married."

Nicholas and his fiancée, Alice, had insisted that Dorothy play piano for their wedding. They'd requested contemporary music, although Dorothy had also brought along her favorite classical pieces. What wedding guest wouldn't be stirred to stand when they heard J.S. Bach's "Jesu, Joy of Man's Desiring" for the bride's processional march?

Mrs. Addyson stepped back. "And you're still tall and as pretty as a peppermint parfait. You haven't changed a bit."

"Thank you." Dorothy ran a hand down her brown braid. "You haven't changed either."

Kindness beamed from the elderly woman's crystal blue eyes. "I'm ten years older and infinitely wiser." Her salt and pepper hair had grown a little grayer, had been cut a little shorter.

Dorothy shaded her eyes and peered toward the street. "Did the music store close? When I drove by I noticed the building was vacant and a 'For Sale' sign was on the door."

"Yes, Musically Yours went out of business about a year ago."

Dorothy well remembered racing into Musically Yours on Saturday afternoons, fingering the darkening edges of well-loved classical pieces that emitted a scent of paper and leather-bound volumes of first edition music.

All the memories brought a sense of familiarity. In Cherish, people knew your name. She'd missed those things because she found city folks indifferent and uncompromising.

The comfortable warmth of the South Carolina sun hit her face, and her heart felt full for the first time in a long time. She gazed at Memorial Street Church's magnificent steeple with the cross on top, and sadness flickered, disrupting the fullness in her heart. She'd hoped to become so much more than a panic-stricken performer who'd relied on opiates for pain. Despite her brief fame, she'd come back to Cherish with her solitude bigger than ever.

It serves you right, her conscience chattered. *You were a fake in high school, forever seeking approval from your classmates to ensure your popularity. Music became your life, your escape, although you're not great at making music anymore, either.*

"Don't bring your issues to church; bring them directly to God," one of her favorite pastors had once said.

She pushed the steely composure of a seasoned performer into place as Mrs. Addyson hooked an arm around Dorothy's shoulders and led her inside. "I always told your late mother you had an ear for music, honey." She gestured upward to the shiny ebony grand piano in the choir loft. "Is Ryan meeting you here so you two can rehearse?"

Dorothy hesitated. "Ryan who?"

"Ryan Edwards. He and your brother were good friends in high school. He'll be singing the Ave Maria at the wedding ceremony during the offering of the gifts. You're his accompanist."

Dorothy's mouth trembled with surprise.

Ryan Edwards.

She tipped her head back and briefly closed her eyes, visualizing Ryan's skinny build, his quiet demeanor, his booming operatic voice which had prompted his high school classmates to snicker. Often he'd accompanied her to Musically Yours, tendering kind support, encouraging her appreciation of Bach and Beethoven and Mozart. And when he would visit her house, Ryan would bring his precious LP's he'd kept hidden in his room and play Luciano Pavarotti and Placido Domingo recordings for her.

Their friendship had grown, and by the time she'd reached her early teens, she'd had a mad crush on him. He'd never known because she'd kept a cool demeanor around him. He was the high school nerd, and her popularity was at stake. In hindsight, she was glad she'd never let on how she felt about him because by her high school sophomore year, he was gone.

"He's become a well-known opera star in Europe and has flown all the way from Italy at your brother's request. Imagine, two famous musicians in our Lord's house." Mrs. Addyson gave Dorothy's shoulder a slight bump and added a mischievous grin. "When he was younger, that boy got into just enough mischief to make him interesting. Bless his heart considering his family was so poor, his Sunday supper was little more than fried water. We're mighty proud of all he's accomplished. He's a few years older than you, so you may not remember him."

"He was my best friend," Dorothy murmured. She set her music briefcase on a back pew and rubbed her forehead. "Nicholas mentioned nothing about Ryan singing."

"These days, your brother is busy between getting ready to graduate from the police academy and the wedding plans. It must've slipped his mind." Mrs. Addyson peered up and read the clock in the choir loft. "Ryan was supposed to be here at one o'clock and he's obviously running late, unless he's canceled altogether and sent a replacement singer. I won't detain you any longer."

"Thanks. I'll get started then."

"Don't forget dinner at The Garden Terrace tonight for the pre-wedding celebration." Mrs. Addyson winked and patted Dorothy's arm. "Your brother said he's treating everyone."

"I wouldn't miss *that* first for the world."

Now if she could only get herself to sit down at the piano and play something.

She willed her heart to stop pounding, willed her pulse to stop racing.

Grimacing, she managed a smile. "See you tonight, Mrs. Addyson."

You have nothing to prove to anyone but God, and he's not judging. The thought came quick through Dorothy's mind.

Taking a long swallow, she made her way up the stairs to the choir loft.

CHAPTER TWO

*R*yan Edwards should've been grinning. The flight from Italy to Atlanta had gone smoothly. The train ride to Cherish was fast and efficient. The Cherish Hills Inn where he was renting a room was well-kept, and he'd managed the short hike from the inn to the church at a brisk pace.

Still, he was late. He knew he was late and there was nothing he could do about it. Returning from a quick jog in town, he'd just had time to shower and change, grab his music bag and come to a short rehearsal. Hopefully the jog would clear his head and help him sleep. He hadn't slept well in months.

Studiously, he kept his head down and ignored the Goodwill Shop and Cherish Sunday Sentinel. Too many difficult memories echoed in these recognizable streets. It was hard enough to enter Memorial Street Church, knowing he hadn't attended a service in years. God had never shown interest in a misfit guy like him.

As a result, he'd made numerous wrong choices. Early on he'd determined what he'd wanted to achieve and had sought the options that suited him best. All people make choices they'd wished they hadn't. Everyone.

And was that God's fault? Guilt nudged.

Perhaps God wanted to help Ryan. Perhaps he should take ownership of his mistakes. Perhaps it was his own fault for resisting.

Nope, he was under too much stress to mull those thoughts around.

He set his jaw and increased his stride, staring straight ahead at the familiar South Carolina landscape—the rolling hills and thick hardwoods and sturdy pine trees. He'd worked hard for his success.

So why was he constantly feeling so fatigued?

He didn't need to prove anything to anyone though he'd secretly relished returning to Cherish to show the towns-people how much he'd accomplished. He was no longer the kid from the poor side of town whose father had killed himself ... a kid to be pitied. Now people looked up to him.

The previous day, he'd received a jolt of surprise when he'd learned that Dorothy, Nicholas' younger sister, was Ryan's accompanist for the wedding ceremony.

Memories of her as a teenage girl brought to mind her spirit, her prettiness, her resolve to be the best at everything she undertook. At fifteen, she'd been gussied up all the time, interested in the latest hairstyles and clothes.

He'd realized that she'd just wanted to fit in.

Didn't we all? At least she'd enjoyed the love of two devoted parents and an older brother. Ryan had no one left except his commode-hugging, knee-walking drunk of a grand-father. His mother had passed away soon after he was born.

He pushed away the disheartening judgments, his thoughts returning to Dorothy. She was an interesting contrast between beauty queen and a homebody, with a streak of tom-boyishness thrown in for good measure. His mouth watered just thinking about her homemade pecan pie —sweeter than stolen honey. She was a one-of-a-kind jewel, and acceptance followed her everywhere. And with the dogged way Dorothy went about things, she was most likely a competent pianist, and the entire run-through of the wedding music would take under an hour.

Despite the warmer weather being a month away, Ryan debated about stopping at Whitney's ice cream for frozen yogurt as he hurried by. Glancing at the time on his cell phone, he thought better of it and kept walking. At three o'clock, he'd arranged a conference call with his agent about a coveted opera role.

"Here he is, our opera star," Mrs. Addyson announced to no one except a hound dog sleeping in the sun, when Ryan arrived a few minutes later. "I'm tickled I got to see you before I left. My Chrysler's parked around the corner."

"Afternoon, Mrs. Addyson." With a brief nod, Ryan executed his most charming smile and made his way up the church steps. "How are you?"

"Fine as a summer morning." She tipped her head. "It's been ten years of Sundays since I last saw you and you've become as good-looking as a Hollywood movie star."

"Thanks, and you're still pretty as a supper of cherry pie." He chuckled, leaned forward, and greeted her with a cheek kiss. He almost reached up to tip his baseball cap before realizing he wasn't wearing it. He grinned. Southern habits die hard. "Ten years goes by fast," he added.

"And you abandoned your hometown for a fine career in Europe."

"Italy is where the opera opportunities are, ma'am."

She tied a royal-blue silk kerchief around her hair and the breeze sent her kerchief fluttering. "Are you joining us for dinner tonight?"

Ryan took in everything—the stately church steeple, the

stained-glass windows reflecting Mrs. Addyson's well-taken-care-of Southern features. When his father had died, she'd come to his house bearing kind words and a funeral casserole. When her husband had passed not long afterward, he'd attended the service—the last time he'd set foot in a church. Since then he'd looked for a sign from God, an invitation to return. The more he searched, the quieter God had become.

Ryan returned her gaze. "The Garden Terrace's restaurant at eight. I received the memo and I'm looking forward to seeing Nicholas and Alice."

"We can thank the good Lord for bringing us all back together."

With sublime effort, Ryan forced himself to nod in agreement and entered the church. The scent of incense and candles and musty hymnals made him pause. He exhaled and pressed the heel of his hand to his temple. Yes, too many memories.

Lifting his music bag, he went through the contents and frowned. In his preoccupation to prepare for his agent's phone call, he'd forgotten the "Ave Maria" back at the inn.

No matter. He'd read off Dorothy's music, assuming she'd brought all the pieces her brother and his fiancée had chosen.

As Ryan shrugged off his charcoal-gray pea coat and headed up the stairs to the choir loft, he expected to hear the sound of the piano. Beethoven's "Fur Elise," perhaps, or "Pachelbel's Canon in D." Instead, a beautiful woman sat curled up in a wooden chair with her legs tucked beneath her. Her ear was pressed to a cell phone, her voice sounded strained. She held up a finger to Ryan and mouthed, "One minute."

Dorothy Thompson.

Spirited and lovely as a teen, she'd also been elusive, which was one of the many reasons he'd admired her. He'd watched the way she'd dealt with her friends. She'd listened to their over-the-top compliments with a grin that was part amused skepticism and part gratefulness.

His breath caught. He simply stared.

Nature had partnered with the years. Her lovely face had realized all of its teenage potential. Thick black lashes fringed vivid eyes which changed from emerald-green to deep Scottish thistle depending on her mood. Her figure was still slim and had filled out in all the right places.

She'd abandoned her black high heels, set neatly on the floor beside a quilted jacket. With her hair pulled off her forehead into a gleaming braid cast over one shoulder, and preferring to go barefoot, she presented a captivating contrast between innocence and maturity.

His little Dorothy had grown into a gorgeous woman, breathtaking with shimmers and sparks.

Nope. Don't go there.

He stopped in mid-stride as cold reality slapped his chest.

He was still reeling from an expensive divorce and a cheating ex-spouse, one performance he had no interest in repeating. Involvement with another woman, any woman, wouldn't be happening again, at least not in his lifetime. Women weren't trustworthy, and achieving a successful career was most imperative. He wouldn't be derailed a second time.

He wanted to be successful. He *would* be successful.

Besides, his conscience annoyed, Dorothy was Nicholas' kid sister.

She talked quietly into the phone, and Ryan grew more impatient when one minute turned to two, then three.

"Are you almost finished?" He glanced at his wristwatch and cleared his throat. "Our rehearsal was supposed to begin at one and I have another appointment at three."

She extended a "thank you, Dr. Gantori," into the phone and clicked off. "And our rehearsal would have started at one o'clock if you were here," she said. "Kindly don't blame me for your tardiness."

He stared into her stormy face, and his lips twitched as her gaze searched his features. "Ryan?" She touched her fingers to her lips. "You've changed."

"For the better, I hope." He leaned back to appraise her shapely form as she came to her feet. "The last time we were together you were doing your best to butcher Mozart's Sonata in C Major."

"And you had perfected an Italian art song, or was it a French mélodie? At any rate, you were preparing to go off to music school on a full scholarship." She cocked her head and smiled. "Oberlin?"

"Juilliard." His gaze flitted over the classical music she'd piled on the piano. "You?"

Her smile wavered. "I'm one of those people who went through high school sporting one image while secretly wanting another."

"Meaning?"

"My mother tried to polish me up to study broadcasting in a prestigious college and marry a rich guy, preferably a billionaire who owned a TV station and several tropical islands. Instead, I practiced my scales and got into a state college. I majored in piano performance."

"You were always so determined. I'm impressed, my love." He'd used that endearment often when they were young, and it just slipped out again, as natural as can be.

Her gaze darted toward the piano. "Was I?" she asked softly.

"I recall you plunking out melodies on Musically Yours' fifty-year-old upright piano."

"You encouraged me ... you can say it now ... my scales required a lot of work." Her smile was quiet. She waited a fraction, seeming to struggle to find the right words. "I got better and learned to read music."

Good. Wisely, he didn't share that thought aloud, wondering how in the world she'd been able to get into a music college. She hadn't begun formal music training until she'd entered high school. However, she'd exhibited remarkable perseverance and had never given up on anything once she'd set her mind to it.

"Well, we're burning daylight when we should rehearse," he said.

With a firm swallow, she pulled on her black high heels and moved slowly toward the piano.

He set down his music bag. "I brought every piece of music on Nicholas' list except the Ave Maria. In my hurry I forgot it in my room."

Dorothy ran her hand along the curves of the grand piano. "You forgot to bring the only piece you're singing?" She plucked a piece of sheet music from her stockpile and took a seat on the piano bench.

"I'm a busy man." He pulled an empty chair from the corner and came to sit beside her. "Do you know the chords for the Ave Maria?"

"No. Do you?"

In the past, her lovely eyebrows would have arched with a look daring him to dispute her. That look would have been preceded by a list of reasons why he should abandon his practice schedule for an impromptu Frisbee toss in her backyard.

Not this time.

"Can't you improvise?" he countered.

"Perhaps." Rolling her shoulders, she blew out a short breath and looked down at the closed piano lid. "What do you want to rehearse first?"

He massaged his temples. "'The Ave Maria.'"

"Of course." She gave a self-deprecating laugh and seemed to withdraw into herself. "What are we waiting for?"

You, he wanted to say. He glanced at his wristwatch, then at her lovely downturned profile.

"Unless you'd like to begin with another piece," he added.

She placed the music for "The Lord's Prayer" on the piano. "Can you sight-read this?"

"I've learned a lot in ten years, Dorothy. I'm interested in hearing what *you've* learned."

Her lips pressed together, and she didn't reply.

With a decisive snap, he lifted the piano lid and propped it up. "Shall we begin?"

With a slight nod, she placed her hands on the keys.

Now why, he pondered before pulling his gaze toward the music, were her hands shaking?

CHAPTER THREE

*R*yan's voice was extraordinary.

Dorothy kept her head down and feigned busyness as she closed the lid of the grand piano. He was a gifted artist, and she was moved by the nuances in his deep bass tone and his incredible vocal range. She'd tried not to glance behind her shoulder and gape while he'd sung the moving lyrics of "The Lord's Prayer." His warm breath had grazed the back of her neck, his rich, dark timbre creating a poignant setting for praising God.

And yes, his virtuoso range had flustered her while she'd played, and she'd halted more than once. Who wouldn't be flustered accompanying a soon-to-be household name in the world of opera? If he'd noticed her hands shaking, he'd politely ignored it.

At eighteen, Ryan had been on the lean side of slim and wiry. Now at over six feet tall, his jaw was firmer, the angles of his cheekbones more pronounced. Gaiety had dimmed from his dark-eyed gaze after his father had died. Afterward, Ryan had become more rebellious, hardly spending any time at the home he'd shared with his drunken grandfather.

She glanced at him, idly wondering if his dark brown hair still took on splashes of gold from the hot South Carolina sun in the summertime.

She'd resisted the impulse to massage her aching right wrist while she'd played and had tried not to grimace whenever she'd reached an octave. Under no condition would she have a panic attack in front of Ryan. She still recalled his admiring glances when they were younger.

His dark eyebrows had lifted whenever she'd held in a moan. She'd controlled her shallow breathing and focused on the impressive vocal range of his bass voice. He made it look so easy.

"Are you sure you're not sick?" he'd asked more than once. "Perhaps you're tired after your long flight from New York."

"I lifted my suitcase in and out of the rental car one too many times." She'd forced a cool dismissal and kept her hands poised on the keys. "Shall we continue?"

His forehead had creased although he said nothing else.

Now that their rehearsal was finished, she grabbed the water bottle from her purse and took a sip, pondering how long it would take to shop for a few groceries at Cherish Country market—beginning with a box of herbal tea, fresh fruit and a bottle of ibuprofen. Probably not enough time, she amended, glancing at the choir loft clock. Check-in at the inn was four o'clock, and then she needed to get ready for the pre-wedding dinner party.

She twisted the cap back on her water bottle and nixed groceries altogether.

With a quick push to her feet, she went to grab her briefcase. She rounded the corner of the piano bench and let out a gasp when she slammed into Ryan's hard chest.

His cell phone was pressed to his ear.

Quickly, he pocketed his phone. His large hands caught her forearms. "Sorry, Dorothy. I wanted to be sure I hadn't missed a call from my agent." The warmness of his long fingers tingled her skin. She stared back into his intense dark eyes and lowered her lashes. If she were honest, he'd completely disarmed her since he'd walked into the choir loft.

She gave herself a stern reprimand. She was being both imprudent and fanciful, much like when she was a dreamy-eyed teen. A couple years back, Nicholas had mentioned that Ryan had gotten married, although she hadn't noticed a wedding band on Ryan's finger.

"No worries, Ryan. Or should I call you Mr. Edwards?" Her voice lowered a fraction. "You're a celebrated artist now."

"Someday, perhaps, if I continue to work hard." His smile came easy, along with a lazy warmth in his gaze. "Here in Cherish I'm Ryan, your best friend. Remember when you'd race me to the Cupcake Escape for a salted triple-caramel cupcake?"

"And you used to let me win."

"And then we would share a cupcake, my love."

My love. Best friends. A million years ago.

He'd departed for college and never contacted her again. Did he know he'd taken a chunk of her adolescent heart with him?

"You're too fancy for any dare now. Look at you, wearing your well-fit clothes, sporting your Rolex watch." She laughed a little, bantering. "Nicholas told me your wife's father owns a large hotel chain all throughout Europe."

"I've been divorced for over a year." Ryan lifted a palm with a "who cares" attitude. "And if I ever become uber-rich, it'll be because of me and my merit."

Some part of her brain processed his information, and she lingered, feeling strangely comforted. He was no longer married.

"I didn't mean to rush up from the piano bench," she continued. "I was thinking about going to the market for groceries, then checking into the place I'm staying and taking a quick shower before dinner."

She felt her face heat as she pushed a reasonable explanation into her voice.

Ryan's grip on her forearms tightened. "We're having dinner at The Garden Terrace tonight, right?"

"Yes. I assume you're invited, too." Unable to stop her steps, she moved a little closer and stared up at him.

The air between them stalled, the seconds beating a steady pulsing rhythm.

"I'll walk you outside." He hesitated before releasing his hands. "Where are you staying?"

"The Cherish Hills Inn. You?"

"Me too."

"Really?"

"Really." He threw back his head and laughed, then opened his arms. She collapsed against him with a chuckle, her cheek pressing against the solid thudding of his heart.

He'd worn a gray cotton polo shirt and black fitted jeans to the rehearsal. His dark-brown hair curled to the collar of his shirt, and her fingers were restless, wanting to brush her hands against his hair. He was the most attractive man she'd ever seen.

She pulled out of his arms and stepped back.

What on earth was she thinking?

The last guy she'd dated, an egotistical violinist, was so vain that she'd been surprised he didn't break his arm patting himself on the back after a successful performance.

No more self-centered musicians, she'd vowed. Especially one who was an obvious rising star.

Was that the reason Ryan's marriage had failed? Was his high-profile career worth more to him than his personal life?

She gave herself a strong mental shake. Neither was any of her business and she wouldn't pry. She wasn't waiting for a relationship with a man to feel worthwhile because she'd learned to rely on herself. Besides, her feelings for him in the past were best left in the past.

Deliberately, she pressed any further thoughts of Ryan Edwards from her mind.

CHAPTER FOUR

*T*he conversation level at The Garden Terrace's restaurant dimmed to a murmur when Ryan and Dorothy strolled in. Ryan was the main draw, the local celebrity, though he seemed oblivious to any commotion he was causing. He looked impossibly good-looking in black pants, a button-down white sport shirt and a gray pea coat that hugged his broad shoulders.

She sniffed appreciatively as he helped her off with her jacket. Scents of grilled chicken and fall-off-the-bone barbecued ribs smoked over mesquite wood tempted her.

"Smells good, doesn't it?" He drew her hand through the crook of his arm "I'll check our jackets at the coat-check. I assume we'll go back to the inn together." He covered her hand with his warm fingers and winked. "Thanks for giving me a lift to the restaurant tonight, roomie."

"We may be at the same inn, but we're not roomies," she corrected. "I'll drive you back if you promise to treat me to a piece of The Garden Terrace's sugar-free lemon cake."

"You brother is treating tonight. I'll take a raincheck."

She nodded, still shaking her head they'd rented rooms at the same inn, on the same floor. There wasn't an abundance of rentals in Cherish, and despite the fact her brother had offered his apartment, it was small and cramped.

Across the crowded dining room, she noted that Nicholas had pushed from his chair and was starting toward them.

Tears sprang to her eyes when her six foot, blond-haired brother reached her. He was a source of inspiration, a true believer in God, and his faith through their daily phone calls while she'd been ill had empowered her to persevere through the nightmarish days of her withdrawal—the vomiting and insomnia and night sweats.

"Don't worry about your career. Your true calling will show up where you least expect it," he'd reassured her. "Your realizations are within your reach."

She hadn't figured out what those realizations were yet, although she'd checked herself into a residential recovery program in New York City the following day.

"It's been too long," Nicholas was saying. "Dorothy, how's the pain? I was beyond worried and prayed hard for your recovery." She couldn't help noticing the husky emotion in his voice.

Beneath her fingers, she felt the muscles in Ryan's forearm harden.

"What recovery?" he murmured.

Evading Ryan's inquiring gaze, she replied to Nicholas, "Prayers are always appreciated."

She pulled her hand from Ryan's arm and scanned the busy restaurant—the wood-beamed ceiling, the various kinds of deer antlers lining a wall, a South Carolina flag hanging across another wall, the waiters and waitresses carrying heaping plates of brisket and onions. She'd always loved the down-home, rustic interior of The Garden Terrace.

"Nicholas, where's Alice?" she asked.

"An emergency at St. Luke's hospital caused her to work later than expected. That's been happening a lot. We're getting married and I hardly see her. I've been in charge of most of the wedding planning." Nicholas pressed his lips tight, then took Dorothy's fingers in his. "In the meantime, I'll introduce you to the wedding party. The wedding is small —a Best Man and the Maid of Honor. Alice's five-year-old daughter is the flower girl. After the ceremony we're having a small reception in the church's basement."

Dorothy nodded. "I'm sure the wedding will be lovely." She didn't know much about Alice except she'd been married twice before and had one daughter. Nicholas and Alice had only been dating a few months, and Dorothy had been surprised when Nicholas had announced their wedding plans so soon.

Ryan placed a light hand on Dorothy's back while they followed Nicholas to a round wooden table in the corner. Mrs. Addyson sat with a group of smiling men and women whom Dorothy thought she vaguely recognized.

"Have you been sick, Dorothy?" Ryan murmured, slowing his pace to detain her. "Is there something you're not telling me?"

"Nothing of interest." She shrugged and took a small step away from him. "Thanks for asking. I'm handling it."

"I'm here if you need anything."

His words hung amidst a background of dishes clattering and people talking. Unexpectedly, a wave of desolation surged through her for all those lost years between them.

Realizing he was waiting for an answer, she blurted, "Are you? You're here for what—a week—before you disappear again for ten years?"

"What's that supposed to mean?"

"Nothing."

He let out a heavy sigh. "I was offered a full scholarship to one of the most prestigious music colleges in the country. I was eighteen and needed to leave this town. I wanted more, and somehow I sense you're angry at me for my decision."

"You always wanted to be on top and you've achieved your goals."

"Have I? Don't presume what you don't know. You're the one who had the world simpering at her feet."

She arched an eyebrow and added a glare. "Who's presuming now?"

He rubbed the back of his neck and lowered his tone. "Look ... I've missed you, Dorothy, all right? I've thought about you a lot. You were only fifteen when I left and I couldn't allow myself to ..." His gaze drifted over her features, lingering on the top button of her ivory silk shirt before focusing on her lips.

"Dorothy!" Mrs. Addyson waved from a wooden table in the corner of the restaurant. "I've saved you a seat next to me and ordered you and Ryan a glass of sweet tea."

"Thanks, Mrs. Addyson." Dorothy glanced over and beamed a smile. When she turned back to Ryan, he was watching her with undisguised interest. "Ryan, I—"

"Go." He directed a meaningful glance toward Mrs. Addyson. "I'll check our jackets and then join you."

When Dorothy reached the table, Mrs. Addyson drew her down to sit beside her. Their table faced a large window with a wide frame.

"This is such a pretty night for a pre-wedding party, it's a shame the bride isn't able to attend," Mrs. Addyson said.

"Nicholas mentioned that Alice is working at the hospital and would be late."

Mrs. Addyson's gaze flicked upward. "The girl's got more

twisted excuses than a pretzel factory." Her tapered, polished pink nail tapped her iced-tea glass. "I'm so pleased to see you and Ryan together again. You two always got along so well, and I know how much you missed him when he went off to college. For weeks afterward you looked like you were eating sadness by the tablespoon."

Dorothy took a sip of her sweet tea, then placed her napkin on her lap. "A lot has happened since we were teenagers."

He'd become successful with a flourishing career and knew where he was headed. She'd gotten sandpapered by wrist pain that had ended her profession before it had begun.

"The Bible says 'For everything there is a season.'" Mrs. Addyson's freckled hand came down to rest on Dorothy's arm. "This is the season for you and Ryan to become reacquainted."

Perhaps, though a week went by extremely fast, Dorothy mused, toying with her delicious sugar-free lemon cake two hours later. By ten o'clock, the long day coupled with nagging wrist pain was taking its toll. Despite Ryan's relaxed posture and light-hearted conversation, she could think of nothing else except returning to the inn for another dose of pain medication, followed by a long soak in the luxurious tub, then lounging in the king-size bed.

She pondered logging onto her laptop and checking the asking price of Musically Yours, the vacant music store. Mrs. Addyson had mentioned the former owners had lowered the price and were actively looking for offers.

Contemplating the possibilities of opening her own music store, Dorothy stared out the restaurant's window at the full moon lighting a starlit sky.

She didn't have more than a hundred dollars in her savings account and she doubted any bank would give an out-of-work pianist a business loan.

Murmuring to Ryan that they should leave, she placed her fork on her dessert plate. She should rest for the two-hour practice the following morning with the rugged, dark-haired man who'd sat beside her all evening, teasing her in his deep voice, his muscled leg casually brushing against hers.

CHAPTER FIVE

*A*t nine o'clock the following morning, Ryan strode down the carpeted hallway of the Cherish Hills Inn and tapped on Dorothy's door. "Ready?" he prompted, when she opened the door and invited him into her room.

"I'll get my jacket." She was dressed in a pair of rich-navy twill ankle pants, a slouchy burgundy sweater and brown suede ankle boots. Her room was feminine, an understated floral scent lingering in the air. He smiled, finding comfort in the fragrance he remembered from long ago.

"I need to be finished by noon," he said. "I'm expecting a call from my agent."

"Again?" She favored him with a smile and an exaggerated, knowing nod. "Don't tell me—let me guess. Another important phone call."

Affectionately, he rumpled her shiny hair that hung loose and wavy down her shoulders. She'd taken down the twisted braid from the previous day, and he felt the desire to snatch her in his arms and kiss the smiling mischief from her lips.

This was the fun-loving Dorothy he appreciated, and he

was gratified by the knowledge he'd put a chink in the cool wall she'd erected when they'd rehearsed.

"My agent is confirming the audition date in Palermo for Verdi's opera *Don Carlos*." Ryan hoisted his music bag over his shoulder. "The competition is aggressive. Jack Youngston, an upperclassman of mine when I attended Juilliard, is also interested in the role."

"With a voice like yours, you'll get the part."

"Jack is very, very good." Ryan twisted the top button of his pea coat. "I'm only thirty and considered young in the competitive opera world. My voice is still maturing and the role of Philip is challenging. Jack is a few years older and his experience is broader than mine."

She grabbed her jacket and Ryan draped it around her shoulders. "I'm not familiar with the opera, *Don Carlos*."

"I played the recording for you a long time ago," Ryan said, insisting on carrying her briefcase. "In the role, Philip evolves from a tyrant to a long-suffering husband."

They advanced to the lobby and nodded to the white-haired innkeeper behind the reception desk who looked up from his newspaper and extended a greeting.

The hum of a television in the parlor brought back images of Ryan's father sitting night after night staring blankly at the same black and white sitcoms. Years before that, his father had invited Ryan to watch Westerns with him.

John Wayne. Memories of popping popcorn with his father on their old gas stove.

A person missed the oddest things after losing someone. Little things.

He gazed at the heartwarming stacked rock fireplace in the parlor and pulled in a breath, ambushed by remembrances of his father's struggles with the demons in his head before he'd taken his own life. He'd hanged himself from a bed sheet noose tied to a wooden rafter right in the middle of their living room while a cheerful fire had burned in the grate and canned laughter had come from the television. Ryan had been the one to find him.

Afterward had been a blur. When Ryan emerged from the deep fog of grief and disbelief, he'd realized he had no choice. He had to get away from Cherish and somehow, some way, climb to the top. He needed a fresh start and looked toward the day when he'd turned eighteen.

Repeatedly shaking his head, he twisted the lion signet ring on the pinky finger of his right hand, the only keepsake he'd kept from his father's possessions.

"That ring was your dad's." Dorothy regarded him. "You've worn it every day since his death?"

"Yes."

She offered a quivery smile and lightly placed her fingers on his sleeve. "I know how much he meant to you. He was a good father."

"Yes."

In the beginning, perhaps.

Ryan wiped at the tears prickling his eyes, aware of the familiar knot settling in his gut. Bleakly, he continued to stare at the enormous fireplace.

She stared at the fire with him, offering silence and her presence.

After several beats, she asked, "And what happens next in *Don Carlos?*"

He didn't answer for a moment, silently thanking her for changing the subject. Taking a long breath to control his voice, he guided her to the entry door and opened it. "Near the end of the opera, Philip laments his loveless marriage and loneliness."

He could empathize with the sorrow, the resignation, the emptiness of a man like Philip. No matter where Ryan searched, he never felt fulfilled.

He swallowed and dragged his thoughts away from that fateful night and all the fears it had brought.

"You'll have to fake the loneliness part," Dorothy said, a tiny smile emerging. "When you're popular you're never lonely, and from what I read about you last night on the internet, you're a household name in Europe."

The knowledge she'd been checking up on him made him grin. "So your philosophy is if you're popular, you're never lonely?"

She avoided his gaze. "My mother's saying."

"Was she right?"

"When I was a teen, I grew resentful of my mother, although I've learned to look at situations differently and now have a different perspective." Dorothy slowed her steps. "I've prayed about our relationship and believe she was getting my life confused with her own."

"So God gave you an answer and your problems and reservations were fixed?"

"Nothing changed." Dorothy tapped her fingertips together. "My faith gave me the sight to understand. God's response gave me a new way to see my situation. My mother wasn't overbearing; she was simply being a mom and therefore engrossed in what she believed was in my best interests."

"For example, doing all she could to ensure you were prom queen in your senior year?"

"You heard?" She smiled. "You were well gone by then."

"Thanks to your brother," Ryan amended, "I kept up with more news about you than you'll ever know."

Her gaze narrowed into a pensive frown. He'd noted she'd asked for clarification while she played in their rehearsal, seeming to look at him for assurances. He offered a smile.

Inwardly, he was concerned.

"Please continue. We were talking about your mother," he reminded.

She looked toward the street. "When I complained to Nicholas about our mother, he would say 'look again.' So I did. And then I'd complain, and he'd say 'keep looking.' His faith in God is tremendous."

"Your brother's an awesome guy. I hope Alice is the right person for him."

"I haven't met her yet."

"Neither have I." Ryan chuckled. "Does she exist?"

"With any luck we'll get to meet her before the wedding." With a wry grin, Dorothy regarded her rental car parked at the curb. "Why don't we walk to the church? The weather is gorgeous."

He supported her suggestion with a chuckle and clasped her hand. One block later, they went by Whitney's Ice Cream. The posted sign in the window stated an eleven o'clock opening time.

Despite their quick stroll, Dorothy stopped to peer at the purple and yellow pansies blooming in wooden planters outside Cherish Styles and Clips. "I love flowers, especially bluebonnets." She bent her head, sniffed, then grinned up at him. "Often I think about the times when we'd skip stones across the open stream near the abandoned railway line. The bluebonnets grew so cheerful along the train tracks and always made me happy."

His lips twitched. "From what I recall, we shared a sling-shot to snap petals off those cheerful bluebonnets." They started forward and their laughing gazes merged.

The air smelled fresh and clean, and the morning sky blurred from dusky rose to a clear blue. Soon a glowing sun would raise the humidity level. This particularly perfect day sent a stab of homesickness right through him. Nothing beat a spring day in South Carolina.

"Last night at dinner while you were talking with your brother, Mrs. Addyson told me you're a concert pianist in

New York City." Ryan tightened his fingers around hers. "Where have you performed?"

"Here and there," Dorothy said dismissively. "You won't be seeing my name on the Carnegie Hall marquee any time soon."

"Why not? Your piano ability at rehearsal was excellent."

She didn't answer and kept her gaze fixed on the sidewalk.

"Will you be returning to New York after the wedding?" he prompted.

She glanced down at their linked hands. "You ask a lot of questions."

"I have undisputed rights to ask all the questions I please because I'm your best friend." They rounded the corner to a local coffee shop. "Coffee?"

"Sure."

"I'll be right back." He placed her briefcase and his music bag near the entrance to the shop and emerged five minutes later carrying a bag with two cups of steaming black coffee poking out of it.

She smiled as he handed her a cup. "Thank you."

"My pleasure."

She gazed up at him, her soft brown hair cascading about her shoulders—so lovely against her flawless complexion and pale pink lips. He studied her for a long silent beat. The summer she'd turned fourteen, she'd cut her long hair into a short bob to copy the latest hairstyle in a popular teen magazine. Predictably, the other girls in her class had soon followed her example. *Dorothy, the trendsetter.* It had been all he could do to rein in his tongue that summer because he preferred her hair loose and long.

"You remembered I like my coffee black?" she asked.

He grinned. "Yes, because I once admonished you for drinking coffee at such a young age."

"My weakness." She returned his grin and tasted.

"Do you have any other weaknesses?" he asked.

"More than I can count." She slanted him a glance. "You?"

His gaze lowered to her face. She was blushing.

Silently, he pondered the edges of the corner he'd effectively pushed them into, took her coffee from her, and set both their cups and the bag they came in on the sidewalk.

"Only one weakness, my love, and she's standing beside me." He inspected her slender form, the way the color in her face intensified as he continued to stare at her. She looked like a tender delicate flower, framed by the wholesomeness of their charming hometown.

"You're beautiful," he breathed.

Her shimmering eyes widened, enormous in her heart-shaped face, adding to the effect of her sweet beauty. And right there on Memorial Street across from the fountain in the town square, he caught her in his arms. He tipped her chin up, his mouth moving closer to hers.

Slowly bending his head, he kissed her. She hesitated, then kissed him back while his hands shifted protectively around her.

"You're a stunning, desirable woman and I've never stopped thinking about you," he whispered.

"Ryan, I—" She stirred and his arms tightened.

The kiss ended as abruptly as it had begun, and for a lingering second, they gazed at each other. The soft yielding in her eyes, a vivid emerald-green, was as if she had spoken aloud.

She'd felt the same attraction pulling them together.

A breeze rustled the pink and purple blooms of a redbud tree, and overhead a male mockingbird sang the song of every bird except his own.

Despite the exquisite feeling of Dorothy's slim body pressed to his, loneliness invaded Ryan's thoughts. Perhaps if he kissed her again, if they stayed where they were, she'd be able to drive away the aching desolation, the ceaseless tension that had become a part of him.

How could the life he'd chosen cause such a strain? Soon he would have everything he'd dreamed about, and there was no reason for him to feel such sadness. Plenty of people were stressed like tightly coiled springs because of overwork, he rationalized. It was the price a person paid to become a winner.

A red-haired customer balancing two trays of coffee dashed out of the shop, jostling them out of the way. Her sunglasses slipped down her nose and she slid them back up. "Sorry!" she called as she rushed past.

Dorothy blinked up at Ryan. "What was that about?"

"The woman was obviously in a hurry."

"You know that's not what I meant." With a fragile smile, Dorothy pulled from his embrace.

He brushed a kiss on her temple and studied her exquisite face before retrieving their coffee cups. "Shall we continue our walk?" he asked.

She drew an unsteady breath, then considered him before refusing the coffee he extended.

"Do what?"

"Shall we continue our—"

Drawing her delicate eyebrows up, she grinned before racing off. "Last one to the church treats the other person to an ice cream!" she called behind her shoulder.

Hurriedly, he stuffed the coffees into the bag. He seized his music and her briefcase, then bounded after her.

He let out a laugh. She was winning, and that was okay. More important, his old Dorothy was returning, and he liked it.

CHAPTER SIX

The music rehearsal at the church proved smooth and uneventful, moving along much quicker than Ryan had expected. Occasionally he noticed Dorothy's face contort with obvious pain, or her fingers tremble on the piano keys. When he asked, she qualified any discomfort behind a forced laugh and lame excuses.

"I owe you an ice cream." He nudged her shoulder when they were finished, then helped her on with her quilted jacket. "May I remind you the race to the church was unfair?"

"May I remind *you* I won?"

"You left me to dash after you carrying two hot coffees and two heavy bags stuffed with music." He checked his wristwatch. "If you can spare the time, let's stop at Whitney's Ice Cream on our way back to the inn."

She laughed impenitently. "Are you sure you're able to squeeze me in? Your life seems full of important appointments these days."

"Nothing is as important as spending time with you." It was the easy, gentlemanly thing to say, and he said the words aloud. Because it was true. It had always been true. Spending time with her had been one of the most cherished aspects of his life.

She smiled with shy hesitation. "Ryan Edwards, are you trying to charm me?"

He had to fight down the impulse to take her in his arms and kiss her again.

Grabbing their music bags, he placed his fingers beneath the elbow of her jacket and guided her down the choir loft stairs. "I've wanted an ice cream and coke at Whitney's Ice Cream ever since I arrived in Cherish."

In the spirit of relaxed camaraderie, they retraced their path toward the inn, then stood in line behind a steady stream of customers at Whitney's before finding two chairs at an outdoor wrought iron table.

After Dorothy was seated, and she'd slung her purse over her chair, he handed her the ice cream cone and a napkin.

"Strawberry is the only ice cream flavor you've ever chosen." He occupied a chair across from her and bent his head to whisper in her ear. "And you've always shared a bite with me."

"Go ahead." A tantalizing smile curved her lips as she extended her cone and he took a lick. "And you've always ordered peppermint chocolate chip."

"I know you, you know me," he said softly.

She pulled in a sharp breath and cut away her gaze.

They ate in silence, interrupted only by the chittering of two squirrels and the jumbled conversations of chattering customers.

"The pain your brother mentioned last night at the restaurant? How often he'd worried and prayed for you?" Ryan set his napkin down. "You asked me earlier and now I'll ask you. What was that about?"

She concentrated on the last licks of her ice cream cone, dabbed her lips with a napkin, and placed it on her lap. "Typ-

ical musician injuries. Carpal tunnel problems ... you know."
She glanced up at him. "What about you? Have you experienced any injuries from all that singing?"

Good deflection, he thought. Going along with her, he
finished his cone and downed a swig of coke. "I've had my
share. When I was at Juilliard, I attempted a repertoire well
beyond me, and my voice wasn't ready."

"You? The master singer?"

"My voice was maturing. Still is, as I mentioned earlier.
That's why the opera in Italy is important, because it's a
tipping point for my career. I know I'm ready for the
challenge."

"You need not prove yourself, Ryan. Not to anyone."

"Perhaps I need to prove something to myself." Meticu-
lously, he squeezed his napkin into a small ball. "Perhaps I'm
impatient for my dreams to become a reality."

The familiar prod of guilt prompted him to lean back in
his chair and reflect. Perhaps his father wouldn't have
committed suicide if Ryan had been a good son. Perhaps Ryan
should have sought help from a mental health professional
when he'd first sensed his father was ill.

Instead, he'd acted out. Even at an early age, Ryan had
gotten into trouble at school. Nothing major, just childhood
pranks. Still ... was he the reason his father had ended his
own life?

"I'm impatient, too," she said. "And I've always been a bit
headstrong."

"A bit?" He sent her a teasing wink. "You possess an
uncanny ability to fit into any social situation."

"Thanks to my mother."

"Thanks to you. You're fun to be around and your outlook
is always positive. However, I've watched you these past two
days and I know you're in constant pain. Please, Dorothy. I
want to know why."

CHAPTER SEVEN

*D*orothy wrung the napkin in her lap.

Ryan sat across from her. Her Ryan. Her good friend. Her confidante.

Not anymore, she reminded herself. Once upon a time, and only then in her daydreams.

They'd had a silent communication when they were childhood comrades sitting for hours on her back porch on sultry summer nights, watching the sun set into a giant red ball, listening to the cicadas chirp their familiar chorus.

"Dorothy?" Ryan's astute brown eyes assessed her. "We used to tell each other everything."

"Sure, when I was fifteen and the world's ultimate chatterbox. 'Everyone should be quick to listen, slow to speak.'" She recited the Bible verse from James 1:19.

"So you have no interest in talking the legs off a chair anymore?" he teased.

She smiled, then drew her jacket tighter around her.

Around them, the loud drone of customers' conversations seemed to grow unnaturally quiet. Drop by precious drop, she felt her confidence draining away.

Ryan was curious and concerned. He wouldn't rest until he knew the truth, and there was no point in evading his questions any longer.

He was from South Carolina, she assured herself. He had a big heart.

Taking a deep breath, she lifted her chin and met his steady gaze.

"Ryan, you should know ..." Her voice shook and there was nothing she could do to control her trembling. "I'm a drug addict, or rather, the appropriate term is 'opiate use disorder.'"

If he was surprised, he didn't show it. His features remained calm and neutral. He clasped her chilly hands in his sturdy ones. "Are you all right?"

"I'm under a doctor's care."

"What happened?"

"I should have told you sooner ... I know I should have." She glanced at him, but there was no judgment, only concern.

"What happened?" he repeated.

"I was over-practicing and sprained my wrist. The doctor advised rest. I argued there wasn't time because I was preparing for a piano recital at a small college in New York. I begged her for something to get me through the performance." Dorothy pulled from his hold and fiddled with the tassel on her purse. "She prescribed opiates for my chronic pain. I felt light-headed after I took them, but I was so grateful for the relief that side effects didn't matter. I could perform without a glitch."

"You're describing opiates as a miracle drug."

"For me they were, until I became addicted to them." She shifted in the cold chair and brushed at her eyes, wet with tears, then quickly looked away.

"Sounds like the opiates were a nightmare instead of a miracle."

She corrected him with a shake of her head. "In fairness, the drugs weren't the problem. I was. I became addicted because I'm weak. I was never the successful girl you admired ... I'm a sham ... and I've failed as a competent musician."

He opened his mouth to speak, then seemed to think better of it. He grabbed hold of her fidgeting hands and gently brushed a kiss on each palm. He'd given her strength when they were younger by his compliments and encouragement. He was doing the same now.

She licked her lips, and her fingers tightened around his. "I tried to stop several times and felt sick and depressed. Somewhere in my mixed-up thoughts I knew I couldn't quit on my own. That's when I reached out to my brother, and his faith in God guided me on the right path. God spoke, and I listened."

"I'd like to share your faith, Dorothy. I really would." Ryan's lips pressed together. "The God you describe is silent for me."

Shaken by the desolate tone in his voice, her gaze fixed on his prominent cheekbones, the slight dark stubble on his jaw, the stubborn turn of his mouth.

"Nicholas reminded me I was too busy and preoccupied in myself to hear God." She lifted her face to the late morning sunlight, then met Ryan's unfaltering gaze. "If you listen, God is everywhere. He was there for me."

"I've sung *piano*, I've sung *forte*." Ryan hesitated, deliberating. "I thought if I searched hard enough I'd find God in Europe while I performed in world-renowned concert halls. I believed I'd found my purpose on century-old stages."

"And did you find your purpose?"

Carefully, he studied her. "People say opera is an emotional, expressive art form about what matters most."

What matters most.

She gazed at this strikingly handsome man whom she'd

had a mad crush on as a young girl. Her love for him had never died. He was a part of her life. He mattered.

And he hadn't answered her question about finding his purpose. This was obviously a subject he didn't plan to pursue.

"I see," she replied.

"This conversation is about you, not me." He flicked a dark eyebrow upward. "How are you being treated for your addiction?"

"My doctor, Dr. Gantori, and a nurse case manager are providing medication and check-in phone calls. My cravings for the drug are better now."

"Good. You're on the right road." His smile was slow, his fingers still around hers. "When will you be heading back to New York City?"

"Sunday. You?"

"Me too. I've booked a flight from Atlanta to Italy. The audition in Palermo is slated for early next week."

They had less than a few days together left, and the thought filled her with despondency. She turned, withdrew her hands from his, and feigned interest in the stone pavers lining the patio so he wouldn't know her sadness.

"We should head back." He glanced at his wristwatch and pushed back his chair. As they stood, he took her bag as well as his, then slipped an arm around her shoulders. "Another practice at nine o'clock tomorrow morning, then?"

"Let's rehearse a while longer because Nicholas changed the recessional song to 'Signed, Sealed and Delivered' by Stevie Wonder." She buttoned her jacket and indicated that Ryan follow her around the outdoor tables. "Nicholas' music choices are a perfect balance between classical and contemporary."

"That's one way to put it." Ryan gave a bark of laughter. "Signed and Sealed and I'm Yours—a meaningful ending after Nicholas and his elusive fiancée sign the wedding registry."

Dorothy laughed and started for the sidewalk. "I'd like to take a peek in the window of Musically Yours, or rather, what used to be Musically Yours. I understand if you want to go ahead because of your appointment."

He hesitated. "The music store on the corner of Myrtle and Magnolia? Has the store been renamed?"

"Musically Yours went out of business." Her voice grew quiet. "And somehow I can't bear the thought."

"Neither can I." Ryan greeted the news by placing his palm against his heart, then claimed her hand.

When they rounded the corner to the abandoned store front, his face blanched. Although the bushes were trimmed, and the lawn mowed, the store didn't blend in with the other tidy businesses lining the street. The display window, which in the past had showcased popular sheet music as well as guitars, ukuleles, and violins, appeared sadly desolate.

He stared through the grimy window. "There's nothing left?"

"Everything was sold at an auction. The owners are asking $100,000 for the abandoned building."

"Renovations on a place this size will run into thousands of dollars. Then there's music inventory, lots of it, which is only the beginning."

"Don't forget shelving and monthly heat and electricity bills." She shaded her eyes and peered inside. "The listing stated the space is one thousand square feet. For the customer who would patronize this type of store, the square footage seems adequate."

Ryan set down the music bags and tried the doorjamb. It swung open. Dust and months of disuse spilled out at them.

With a roguish grin, he stood back to survey the badly fractured door frame. "Shall we look inside?"

She perused the empty sidewalks. "We can't enter a property without a realtor. Suppose someone sees us and accuses us of stealing."

He added a wink to his grin. "There's nothing in here except an old ukulele missing all its strings." He nodded toward the broken instrument sitting sideways in the corner. "If anyone asks, we're prospective buyers."

"That excuse wouldn't float for a minute. I can't afford this property and you're not looking. You live in Europe."

He nudged their bags inside. "I used to live in Cherish. This is my hometown as well as yours."

She stepped over the store's threshold with him, fingering the well-loved brick on the interior of one wall while studying the numerous nail holes on the others.

"The music was arranged in rows alphabetically by composers," she said. "Remember?"

He indicated the front window. "The gigantic composer of the month statue always made me pause."

Her gaze automatically surveyed every inch of the space she had once spent so much time in. "And the composer's music was piped as background throughout the store."

"When I used to walk by and hear Mozart, it drew me in like a siren."

She nodded and continued toward the rear. "I always thought the owners should offer music lessons. There's a separate entrance so students wouldn't be traipsing in and out, especially if lessons were held after store hours."

"The owners were elderly. They didn't want the hassle."

"There should be more cultural opportunities in Cherish." An unexpected elation built inside her along with a conviction taking root. "There's Memorial Street Church choir and the high school band. However, a music conservatory would fit perfectly into this community and it could begin right here." She gestured toward the back room which the previous owners had used for storage.

"This is a small community," Ryan reminded. "A conservatory and retail store is a large undertaking, and don't forget there's another music store over in Stanley."

"That store is in the next town."

His phone buzzed. He pulled it out of his jacket, glanced at the message and frowned before pocketing it.

"Anything important?"

He smiled into her eyes. "It can wait."

She drank in the mustiness of the air along with the remembrances. "A music store and lessons would feed off of each other, and monthly recitals and concerts could be scheduled." She wiggled her shoulders and faced him. "I'd have an excuse to get all dressed up again."

"The sight of you in a fancy dress would make me want to fly back to Cherish every weekend." He laughed. The deep throaty sound had always made her heart beat double time. Then he sobered, and the amusement was replaced by a languid gaze, keeping her rooted where she stood.

He moved forward. Bending his head, he brushed his lips against hers, the bristle of his stubble sweeping against her cheeks. "You would light up any concert hall," he whispered.

"Me? Hardly." She waved a hand dismissively, stepped back, and kept her voice steady. "Ryan, I know our community would support a music store and conservatory."

He lifted a dark eyebrow. "*Our* community?"

"Yes. You just said this was your hometown as well as mine." She felt her spine get straighter. "You spent your entire childhood here."

He shrugged nonchalantly. "I suppose if one thousand square feet was a good enough space for Musically Yours, then it's good enough for us."

Somewhere in the empty space, she allowed herself a small intake of breath. Swallowing, she stared up at him. "Us?"

"Yes, ma'am." He reached for her, and his lips parted hers for a deep kiss. "Are you looking for a silent partner, my love?"

CHAPTER EIGHT

*D*orothy rubbed her eyes and blinked at the early morning sunlight streaming through her window. Lying in the Cherish Hills Inn's luxurious king-sized bed, she flicked a glance at the time on her cell phone, grateful she could rest another half hour.

She rolled over onto her side and faced the window. Although she courted sleep, her mind was active, and she lifted a prayer to God.

"Christ is with me. His plan for me will come to pass. I believe it will happen because You are in complete control and whatever comes my way, I can handle it. Amen."

As she watched the sun rise, her thoughts turned to Ryan —his recklessly rugged face, his arresting gaze, his admiring smile. A cosmopolitan aura surrounded him, his long strides strong with authority. She'd watched videos of his performances on the internet, and it was clear the audiences loved him. During interviews he'd offered a firm handshake, laughing while he'd accepted lavish compliments from his fans with humility and grace.

A star. A talent to be reckoned with.

She could hardly believe this sophisticated man was the same man who'd raced her to church and shared an ice cream cone with her. Or the young boy who'd held back tears after his father's funeral. He'd tried to push the grief away, push her away. He'd been in crisis and had attempted to close himself off from her.

She knew the feeling well. She hadn't wanted to open up to him because she'd felt inept and unworthy, as if she'd just fallen off a turnip truck whereas he was all bland urbaneness. She was a far cry from the popular girl he'd once admired.

Yet she'd ended up telling him everything about her addiction, including her defeat.

Despite his easy smiles, she sensed he was in crisis too, an internal one which couldn't be assuaged by recognition and wealth. He wasn't being honest with himself. More important, he wasn't being honest with God.

She sighed, knowing that in a few days he would be leaving. On the other hand, she'd decided to begin a new chapter in Cherish where life felt safe and friendly and comfortable.

The previous evening she'd notified her landlord in New York City, who'd graciously agreed to let Dorothy out of her lease at the end of the month. Her handful of friends had offered to pack up her apartment and ship her belongings to Cherish as soon as Dorothy sent a forwarding address. She promised to keep in touch, realizing in hindsight that several friends had negatively enabled her by lending her money when she'd fallen short of funds. She'd needed a greater quantity of the drug as her tolerance increased and her addiction had progressed at a frightening rate. Consequently, she'd exhausted her savings.

However, Emmanuelle, a woman of great faith and Dorothy's closest friend, had offered what the doctor termed "positive enabling." Emmanuelle had encouraged Dorothy to seek therapy and check into rehab. She'd also spoken to

Nicholas in nightly phone conversations throughout Dorothy's recovery.

Dorothy had appreciated her friend's concern. Despite Emmanuelle's brilliant musical career as principal harpist for a prestigious symphony, she was dealing with her own issues. She'd been dating a wealthy man that Dorothy considered controlling, yet Emmanuelle refused to recognize his manipulation. She'd moved in with him and had since fallen off the earth.

Dorothy lifted a prayer to give Emmanuelle the wisdom to end her unhealthy relationship. Then she added praise, knowing He had placed numerous good people in her path. Nicholas, Emmanuelle, Mrs. Addyson and Ryan.

Ryan.

She whispered a 'thank you' for bringing him back into her life. In their few remaining days together, she intended to memorize everything about him—his striking face, his charismatic smile, his good-natured teasing—until his return. Because surely he'd come back to Cherish to confirm that his business investment was sound.

"I won't be able to see the day-to-day operations," he'd said before kissing her good night, "so I'll leave all the decisions in your capable hands."

Then, before she'd retired, he'd texted, 'Sleep tight, I'll be dreaming about you. If anyone can ease my insomnia, thoughts of you can.'

She lifted her left hand and stared at her slim fingers. Perhaps as time went by, she and Ryan would become even closer. Perhaps someday she'd be wearing his engagement ring, followed by a wedding band. Perhaps Ryan had been in her future all along, even when they were teenagers.

She smiled, pushed back the covers and scrambled out of bed. It was time to dress for a picture-perfect day and another exhilarating rehearsal with Ryan.

~

"I've been thinking about your pecan pie for a month of Sundays," Ryan said, looking up from the music he'd been studying. Looking disgracefully handsome wearing a pair of worn denims and a navy T-shirt, he sat on a high stool at Cherish Hills Inn's large center island, his dark eyebrows drawing together as he sipped a glass of sweet tea. Now and then, he'd softly sing the music from Verdi's opera. Then he'd banter with Dorothy as she rolled flour and shortening for pie crust, rousing her into reminiscing about their teen antics. He laughed with her, his tense expression easing, his features almost boyish.

The inn's owner had explained that the kitchen had recently been renovated, painted in light gray and white, offset by black countertops, stainless steel appliances and copper fixtures. The effect was a striking combination between beauty and functionality.

"Dorothy." Ryan slid his index finger around the rim of his iced tea glass. "When you asked me to join you this afternoon in the kitchen ..."

"You said you'd be here with bells on," Dorothy finished.

He chuckled. "And here I am."

"You could've used the time to prepare for your upcoming audition."

"I'd much rather watch you." He studied her as she sprinkled flour onto the dough, kneaded, then picked up the rolling pin. When she was satisfied, she arranged the single-crust dough into the pie plate, then crimped and placed tin foil around the edges.

"It was nice of the owner to let me use his kitchen and oven and utensils," she said.

Ryan reached across the island and gently wiped a flour

smudge from her cheek. "You realize he'll want a piece of pecan pie as payment? If there's any left."

"You can't eat an entire pie by yourself." With an exasperated sidewise glance, she placed her hands on her hips, smearing flour on her denims. "And I'll want to put slices aside for Mrs. Addyson and Nicholas and Alice."

"Speaking of Nicholas and Alice, will they make their home in Cherish?" Ryan asked.

She set the oven to pre-heat. "The wedding is in three days, and I haven't talked to Nicholas since dinner. You?"

"No, not a word." Ryan fanned through several pages of music. Rubbing a hand down his face, he sighed and closed the music score.

"Done?" She flashed him a smile while she resumed setting out the rest of the ingredients for the pie.

"More than done. It's a challenging role and my voice is pushed from high to low extremes." He ran a hand through his hair. "My audition is slated for next Wednesday, which will give me two days to recover from jet lag after I arrive in Italy. You're staying in Cherish, correct?"

"Yes. I've canceled my flight to New York City and will live here at the inn until I find my own place. Ryan ... you'll ... you'll let me know how your audition goes?"

She kept her tone light. She wanted to add, when will I see you again? We have so little time left together.

She said neither.

"You'll be the first person I contact." He checked his phone, then placed it on the island. "I noticed the 'sale pending' sign on the store and received an email from the bank. The closing is in a couple weeks. That's quick."

"It's quick because we're offering a cash deal. Or rather, *you* are. Thank you for your generous offer. Remember, this is a loan and I intend to pay you back."

He stood, poured her a glass of sweet tea from a pitcher

in the refrigerator and set it on the island for her. "I consider Musically Yours a good investment, and I know the store will be a success with you at the helm."

"And you."

"I'm a silent partner. I won't be able to travel to the states often after *Don Carlos* begins production. That is, if I get the role. My agent informed me that Jack Youngston is already in Palermo."

"I'm certain the role will be yours."

"Thanks." He settled on the stool. "Your confidence in my abilities means a great deal."

She whisked together sugar, corn syrup, the rest of the ingredients and chopped pecans. With a flourish, she placed the pie in the preheated oven, set the timer and piled the mixing bowls in the white ceramic farmhouse sink.

"I've written out a business plan for our store." Ryan reached into his jeans pocket and handed her a list as she took a stool across from him. "Purchasing music and supplies is the first step. Eventually, you may want to sell musical instruments. If kids take music lessons at school, they can rent or purchase instruments at the store, which is added revenue."

Perusing the list, she nodded thoughtfully.

"Then choose your specialism," he continued. "Are you planning to teach piano lessons?"

"Absolutely." She raised the glass of sweet tea to her lips. "I believe God was leading me back to Cherish. He had a purpose, and this is my season to do something I was meant to do all along."

"Your purpose ..." Ryan's gaze was probing, his words careful.

"In every situation, there is a purpose. Every struggle, every setback, every incident. God decided my purpose before I had even glimpsed it."

His gaze flitted around the enormous kitchen. "God is here?"

"God is everywhere. You're always standing at a new opportunity if you give it a purpose." She paused, forming the same question on her tongue, the same question she'd asked the other day. "What is your purpose, Ryan?"

He shrugged indifferently. "Success, I suppose."

"Wealth?"

"The money part never interested me." He folded his arms across his chest and leaned back. "After my divorce, my new wealthy friends didn't offer the support system I thought they would. I was finally part of the 'in' crowd after being an outsider for so long. And you know what? I found I didn't like them—their mentalities, their 'never enough' lifestyles."

She nodded and went to the sink, picked up a clean kitchen towel, and wiped down the shiny black countertops. "So what is your purpose, Ryan?" she asked again.

"I don't know anymore, except that I want what you and your brother have—an unshakeable faith, the strength to forge ahead no matter how disappointing the circumstances."

She studied him and reformed her question. "So what has taken all your attention these past ten years? Your driving ambition, or God?"

"I no longer ask God for anything. I've given up because He's never responded."

"How can you expect God to respond if you don't uphold His standards?" she asked softly. "Those so-called friends were pulling you in the wrong direction."

"In hindsight, you're absolutely correct." He stood, then sat, then stood again, striding to the sink, rinsing mixing bowls, placing wooden spoons on the copper strainer to dry. His gaze shifted to her. "Things have been tough for you and you've pulled through."

She set down the towel. "Thanks to a good support system, I was forced to be honest with myself."

His probing gaze met hers and he offered a smile. Then he turned, seeming to stare at nothing for a long moment. "Honesty isn't easy, especially with yourself."

Despite their gaiety a few minutes earlier, she sensed his smile was strained.

Worried about his upcoming audition? Although she wished there was something she could do to ease the dark circles under his eyes, the lack of sleep was evident in his rugged face if one looked closely.

He rounded the island and drained his glass of sweet tea. He set the glass down and turned to her. "Dorothy?"

"The pie isn't done yet." She attempted to deflect his serious tone with an easygoing remark.

He walked toward her, coming to stand within arm's reach. "Did you know the sweet and gooey scent of pecan pie baking in the oven makes me think about one thing?"

"Calories?" she provided with a tongue-in-cheek smile while taking one wary step back. "You'll want to stay trim for your role as Philip."

A warm gleam softened his eyes. Reaching out, he pulled her toward him. "There's another role I'm much more interested in."

"Ryan, the pie—"

He pressed his finger against her lips. "The pie isn't done yet, so we have lots of time." He drew her to him and touched his mouth to hers, coaxing her lips to part. She placed her hands around his nape, feeling the silky hair curling at the back of his neck.

His cell phone rang. Ignoring it, he deepened the kiss.

When his phone rang the second time, she broke the kiss and glanced toward the island.

His dark gaze lit with amusement. His arms around her tightened. "I'm not expecting any calls. Are you?"

"Obviously not." She rested her forehead against his hard chest, her fingers flattening on the rich woven texture of his shirt.

When his phone pinged for a third time announcing a text message, she indicated that he should answer it. "The caller is obviously being persistent."

With a resigned nod, he strode to the island. He read the text message, his expression changing to one of surprise, then disbelief.

She leaned against the counter and fingered the neckline of her red fleece pullover. "What is it?"

"The calls were from my agent. The opera company has moved up the audition schedule." Ryan looked past her, his gaze unfocused. "I need to be in Italy by Saturday."

"Impossible." She rubbed her arms, her thoughts whirling. "Nicholas' wedding is Saturday."

"I ... I'll ... Maybe your brother can change the date ..."

"Of the wedding? For you? You're joking, right? Even *you* can't believe you're that important."

"I don't." His arms fell to his sides. "But this is a major opera and if I don't audition, I won't get the role."

"What about Nicholas and Alice?"

"I'll explain the situation to Nicholas and I'm sure he'll understand. I can ... I can record the Ave Maria ahead of time." Ryan gripped her by the shoulders to face him. "You can play the recording at the church."

She swallowed hard. "What about 'The Lord's Prayer?'"

"Yes ... and 'The Lord's Prayer.' I'll sing the solo a cappella, without your accompaniment. I always bring a portable audio recorder with me." He tipped up her chin and pressed a quick kiss on her temple. "All you must do is hit the play button on Saturday. It's easy."

No, no.

"Of course." She offered a false cheerfulness and pressed a hand on the island to steady herself.

The oven timer beeped. She hitched up her shoulders, grabbed two oven mitts from a drawer and lifted the pie from the oven. "What about the Stevie Wonder song we rehearsed for the recessional?"

"Find a good recording. The original is better than anything we put together."

She winced.

"Dorothy, I'm sorry. You know how much this role means." His voice dropped, his eyes tightened. "I'll book a flight out of Atlanta this afternoon, then go pack."

He was talking on his cell phone, busy with travel arrangements, as she quietly set the pie on the stove and shuffled out of the kitchen.

CHAPTER NINE

*S*aturday came in bright with promise. Dorothy showered and washed her hair, then carefully dressed in a simple black sheath with a scalloped neckline. She decided on an elegant dress in a conservative mid-length, critically appraising herself in the full-length mirror in her room. She straightened the black velvet bow securing her hair smoothly at the nape, the rest falling in soft waves around her shoulders. Tiny diamonds sparkled at her ears and she secured a pearl necklace around her throat.

Despite a lump of anticipation in her stomach, she was ready early for the six o'clock candlelight ceremony, allowing herself plenty of time to warm up with scales and arpeggios before the wedding guests arrived.

The previous evening, Nicholas had phoned to cancel the wedding rehearsal, explaining that Alice had said they didn't need one. After all, the wedding was small with only a Maid of Honor and Best Man in attendance.

"No problem," Dorothy had agreed, shifting her attention to Ryan's list of things to do before opening Musically Yours.

By five o'clock, the sun was beginning its descent as

Dorothy made her way from the inn to her car. She secured a parking spot in front of Memorial Street Church a few minutes later.

For several beats, she sat in the car with her eyes closed.

She'd be performing solo. Suppose her fingers refused to play the rapid eighth notes in Pachelbel's Canon in D? Suppose her wrist hurt so badly while she performed Bach's Jesu, Joy of Man's Desiring, that she couldn't continue?

No. She refused to scare herself with negative thoughts and focused on her aim—contributing to her brother's wedding by giving her best performance.

"Thank you, God, for selecting me for this purpose," she whispered.

Taking a confident breath, she double-checked her briefcase containing her piano music and Ryan's solos. Before he left, she overheard him phone Nicholas to explain why he couldn't perform at the wedding and had ended with a heartfelt apology. As was his character, she knew her brother had wished Ryan only the best.

Ryan had left his recordings on the kitchen island, along with a sealed note addressed to her which she'd found the following morning.

With shaking fingers, she'd opened his note and read:

My love,

I could see it in your eyes you were hurt and disappointed with my choice. I'm sorry. You know how much this role means. I hope you can forgive me and someday give me a chance to make things better between us. You are special and mean so much to me—more than you know.

In his usual bold script he'd signed, *"Love, Ryan."*

She'd installed herself on a stool in the kitchen and stared at the note. Just stared. Tears trickled down her cheeks as she thought of the slim, dark-haired man whom she wouldn't see again for a long, long time. In her dreams she had imagined they might have a future together. Now he was gone, choosing his career over his commitments, his friends, and her.

Without a second thought she knew his success would continue to spiral upward after *Don Carlos* ended, and Ryan's stardom would keep him performing in Europe for years.

They'd never laugh together again. He'd never hold her in his solid arms, never call her "my love" in that tender, affectionate tone he'd used so often.

She'd grasped the note and huddled into herself, whispering a Psalm she knew by heart. "'Weeping may last through the night, but joy comes in the morning.'"

When shadows fell to early afternoon, her tears were exhausted. She'd pushed up the sleeves of her plaid blouse and risen to her feet. Once before she'd been held hostage by her disappointment, her hopes dashed. She wouldn't allow it to define her a second time.

Three days had passed since Ryan boarded the plane from Atlanta to Italy. He'd texted her only once, saying he'd arrived safely and was preparing for his audition.

"Good," she'd texted. "Best of luck."

Now, with her posture strong and her breath purposeful, she grabbed her purse and briefcase. She was well-rehearsed to play her best for her brother and his fiancé on one of the most important days of their lives.

Mrs. Addyson, dressed in a lilac wool suit, stood at the top of the church stairs and greeted Dorothy with a nod. Her usually pleasant demeanor was distraught, and she seemed unnaturally quiet.

"Good evening, ma'am." Dorothy paused at the open wooden door leading into the inside vestibule. "I didn't expect you at church this early."

"Haven't you heard?"

Dorothy scoured her thoughts. "Heard what?"

"The wedding is off." Two bright flushes of red heightened Mrs. Addyson's rouged cheeks. "Alice texted your brother a few minutes ago and broke up with him. She's been seeing another fella at the hospital."

Dorothy set down her briefcase and purse and pulled out her phone. "Nicholas will be devastated." She stared down at her hands, then managed to return Mrs. Addyson's gaze. "Where is he?"

"He's still at his apartment. Most likely he's hurt and embarrassed."

"So there's no wedding?" Dorothy gazed into the church. The pews had been simply decorated with white ribbons. Colorful potted plants sat beneath the church's stained-glass windows.

"It's sad. Fortunately, there aren't a lot of vendors to be paid. Nicholas' friends were all contributing a covered dish for the church reception."

"Do they know?" Dorothy absently looked up from her phone. She'd texted her brother and hadn't received a response.

"I've notified everyone." Mrs. Addyson gave Dorothy a penetrating stare. "And I know your Ryan flew to Italy."

"He's not my Ryan," Dorothy said quietly. "With his talent, he belongs to the world."

"I saw the way he looked at you in the restaurant. I remember the way he looked at you when you two were young." She took Dorothy's hand. "He'll always find his way back to you."

Dorothy's gaze flew to Mrs. Addyson, then slid downward. She shook her head, put her phone away and focused on the church steps. A mixture of loneliness and dejection tore through her—gray and dull—but the delicate hope Mrs. Addyson offered bloomed like a bouquet of colorful flowers.

"Can you wait here at the church until the wedding cake

is delivered?" Mrs. Addyson let go of Dorothy's hand and pulled on her proper white gloves. "My Chrysler is parked around the corner and I'd like to get home before dark. The key-holder will lock up the church later this evening."

"What will I do with an entire wedding cake?"

"Take it back to the Cherish Hills Inn, I suppose. The bakery in town hired a talented new baker. He's a bit temperamental, which is why he might be late."

"Another artist," Dorothy murmured.

"Creative people are complex and sensitive." Mrs. Addyson paused, her anxious gaze riveted on Dorothy. "I can come by tomorrow and share a piece of wedding cake with you. The innkeeper told me you've decided to make your home in Cherish. Welcome back."

"Thank you, ma'am. I'm buying Musically Yours."

"That's as fine a bit of news as cream gravy." Mrs. Addyson beamed knowingly. "Nothing stays secret in a town this size for long, you know." With a nod of her elegantly coiffed gray hair, she bade Dorothy a good evening and made her way down the steps. Soon, walking quickly in her sturdy leather pumps, she disappeared around the corner.

Dorothy seated herself on the church's top step and placed her purse and briefcase beside her. She checked her cell phone, noting her brother still hadn't answered her texts. She'd decided to give him room to come to terms with Alice's actions. Tomorrow if he wanted to talk, she'd listen, digest, reflect and pray with him.

Dusk came sooner than expected, and the roads of Cherish, lit by corner streetlights, took on streaks of silver and gray. Tree branches swayed in wafts of cool air, and a flash of a white tail signaled the bob of a shy rabbit searching for cover. Cars hummed the streets, an intermittent flow of red and white lights.

After thirty minutes passed with no sign of a wedding

cake delivery, Dorothy gathered her belongings and stood. In the morning she'd extend her apologies to the bakery and Mrs. Addyson, for there was little use in waiting for a cake no one would be eating, anyway.

A dark sedan pulled to the curb behind her Ford rental.

Dorothy hurried down the church steps. "Perfect timing!" she called as a man emerged.

He didn't carry a wedding cake. And the sedan tore away from the curb and headed down the street.

She hesitated, debating, smiling uncertainly. Surely the temperamental baker hadn't forgotten to bring his own cake.

Except this tall, impressive man wasn't the baker. This man, who was striding toward her clutching a handful of blue-bonnets and looking like a broad-shouldered handsome opera singer, was wearing a polo shirt and a beige suit jacket. And he was heartbreakingly familiar.

"Ryan." Her briefcase and purse slid from her grasp. She stopped at the bottom of the steps. "What ... what are you doing here?"

"I found my purpose," he said solemnly.

"Purpose?" Her heartbeat raced. A breath wouldn't come. "Where? In Italy?"

"I found my purpose right here in my hometown."

Disoriented by his reply, she avoided eye contact. "Your audition ... did you audition for *Don Carlos*?"

"Yes." He closed the distance and stopped within an inch of her. "My agent arranged the audition as soon as I arrived in Italy."

"So why aren't you ..." She wasn't easily pacified and tried again. "So when will you hear how you did?"

"I've already heard."

"And?"

He drew a long breath and slowly expelled it. "I got the role."

She should congratulate him. And she would as soon as she had the ability to think coherently. "Ryan, I ... I'll watch your performances if they're televised here in the states. I'll applaud you along with the rest of your—"

"I turned it down."

"You *what?*"

"I turned the role down. After my audition I was offered a contract. I thanked my agent and the casting directors, turned around and booked the next flight back to Atlanta."

Her body tensed. Her eyes widened. "I ...I don't understand."

He handed her the bouquet of the delicate, fragrant blue-bonnets, then looked around, momentarily diverted. "Where is everyone?"

"The wedding was called off. Long story." She accepted the flowers and sniffed appreciatively, the fragrance filling the air with a sweet airy scent. "Thank you. Where did you get these?"

"There's an open stream near an abandoned railway line a few blocks from here. You've pointed out frequently that bluebonnets are your favorite, so I picked a bouquet for you."

She fingered the lovely blooms, as delicate as boomtown silk. No store-bought flowers from him. These delicate blue flowers were heartfelt and strong and memorable.

"I didn't expect you to remember that."

"I remember everything about you." The earnestness in Ryan's brown eyes brought a rush of heat to her cheeks. "And now I need to tell you something, Dorothy."

She scanned his face. He was here, but he'd be leaving to go somewhere else, somewhere with brighter and better opportunities.

"What is it?" she asked warily.

"Your faith pushed me toward honesty."

"Ryan, you've always been honest—"

"No, not with myself." His gaze never left hers. They were so close although he made no move to touch her. "Seeing you in a crisis made me take a clear-eyed view of my life. You faced your weaknesses, and your faith in God never wavered. You confronted your failings head-on. I didn't. After my father's suicide I buried my emotions—the anger, the bitterness, the grief—beneath busyness, believing if I could land at the top, I would've achieved my goals."

"You have. You're a—"

"I haven't," he interrupted. "However, on the plane trip to Italy, I dug deeper inside and honestly challenged myself. I'd never done that before."

She considered him, felt the tears standing in her eyes. "And what did you discover?"

Gently, he traced a finger along her cheek. "I found it's much easier to diagnose other people's problems rather than your own. I recognized you were in crisis. What I refused to acknowledge was that I was too."

Puzzled, she looked away. "I don't understand."

"When I saw you again that first day in the choir loft, I almost couldn't breathe. You were barefoot, all curled up on that chair with your legs tucked beneath you, and you were as adorable as a calico kitten."

She leaned back and attempted to speak. No words came.

He placed the flowers on the ground and gazed into her eyes. "You'd grown into the beautiful woman I'd always admired from a distance." He enfolded her into his arms, holding her against his cotton polo shirt. His heart beat solid and reassuring.

"When I was a teenager," she whispered unsteadily against his chest, "I made excuses to be near you. I had butterflies in my stomach every time you were around."

He tipped up her chin. "And now?"

"And now I want to be around you more than ever."

"I thought about you a lot those past ten years." He braced his hands on her shoulders. "Sometimes bits and pieces, along with remembrances of my father—his changes of mood, his agitation. Memories of Cherish, both good and bad, flickered and faded. Seeing you again I realized the good memories had one thing in common."

She attempted a trembly question and swallowed.

"And that one thing was you." His lips moved closer to hers. "Every good memory had you right in the middle of it."

He pressed her closer and her fingers locked around his nape. His lips found hers and he kissed her with a hard, insistent urgency. She returned the kiss with the same earnestness, glorying in the sensation of his mouth, sending spirals of desire clear down to her toes. When the kiss ended, he embraced her face in his hands. Lovingly, his thumbs stroked her cheeks.

Stars twinkled like vibrant crystals in the night sky. The air had turned cooler. Crickets chirped, mingling with a whip-poor-will's chants. Somewhere in the distance, bullfrogs croaked. The sounds of spring, a spiritual promise of renewal, a symbol of new life. Here in Cherish, with Ryan's arms around her, the seeds of growth held promise.

Dorothy leaned her head back and gazed at his full, firm mouth, extending a not-so-subtle invitation to kiss her again.

"If you stare at me like that, I won't be able to finish, and I have more to say." He pressed a kiss on her temple, then murmured against her hair. "I didn't return to Cherish for you. I returned for your brother's wedding."

She gave a rueful sigh and shook her head. "All for naught."

His eyebrows rose. "Was it? Your brother's wedding being canceled makes me realize more than ever that we were both in the right place at the right time." He paused for an interval of several seconds. "Then when I left for Italy, I told myself I had enjoyed our time together and rationalized it was enough."

She stared up at him. "Was it enough?"

"It wasn't enough for me." His gaze was solid and steady. "I love you, Dorothy Thompson. Always have, always will. I'm here because I want you to marry me."

She gaped in speechless joy. She'd racked her brain, trying to think of what she might've done differently to encourage Ryan to stay. Perhaps that day in the inn's kitchen she could have said something, talked with him, implored him. Instead, she'd walked out of the kitchen and left him alone.

And all along, God had planned this reunion. His timing was perfect.

"What about your career?" she asked.

"My career is music. I'll teach vocal lessons and help you open the music conservatory. Together, we'll build Musically Yours back into one of the finest music stores in South Carolina."

"What you're saying ... the store ... the conservatory ... you living in Cherish ... I don't know how to respond."

"I love you back is a good beginning."

"Ryan Edwards, I love you back." She stared up into his earnest expression. "What I have to adjust to is the fact we're really going to get married."

"It's easy. Just say yes."

"Marriage is serious."

He laid both hands on her shoulders. "And I couldn't be more serious."

She shook her head. She needed some place to think. Or did she? Gazing into the face of the man she loved, only one reply formed on her lips.

"Yes."

"Do you mean it?" he persisted.

"I do." Yearning for Ryan's lips on hers, she stood on her toes and slid her arms around his shoulders.

Their hearts now beat in a skillful cadence because God proved that His timing is always perfect.

THE END

A NOTE FROM JOSIE

Thank you for reading *A Love Song To Cherish*. I hope you enjoyed your visit to the scenic town of Cherish, South Carolina, and the music store, Musically Yours.

If you loved this romance as much as I loved writing Ryan and Dorothy's story, please help other people find *A Love Song To Cherish* by posting your review, as well as for the bundle: Romance Stories To Cherish.

This series continues with *A Christmas To Cherish*, featuring Dorothy's brother, Nicholas, and her friend, Emmanuelle, and then A Valentine To Cherish, featuring Scarlett and Christian singer, Joseph. If you love adorable puppies and the holidays, you'll also enjoy the 4th book in the series, A Christmas Puppy To Cherish.

Book Five, A Homecoming To Cherish, brings 2 new characters to town, Nora and Julian. You'll also enjoy Nora's teenage daughter, Samantha.

A Love Song To Cherish is available in ebook, paperback, Large Print paperback, Hardcover, and audiobook.

I'd love to meet you in person someday, but in the meantime, all I can offer is a sincere and grateful thank you. Without your support, my books would not be possible.

As I write my next sweet or inspirational romance, remember this: Have you ever tried something you were afraid to try because it mattered so much to you? I did, when I started writing. Take the chance, and just do something you love.

My Spotify Play List for A Love Song To Cherish is here.

With sincere appreciation,

Josie Riviera

DOROTHY'S PECAN PIE RECIPE

Prep time: 20 minutes
Bake 1 hour

Ingredients

- 1/2 cup sugar
- 3 tablespoons flour
- 1 cup light corn syrup
- 1 cup dark corn syrup
- 3 eggs
- 1 teaspoon white vinegar
- 1/2 teaspoon vanilla extract

- 1 cup chopped pecans
- Pastry for a single-crust pie

Directions

- **1.** In small bowl, whisk sugar, flour, corn syrups, eggs, vinegar and vanilla. Stir in pecans. Pour into pastry shell and place foil around edges.
- **2.** Bake at 350° for 35 minutes. Remove foil; bake 25-30 minutes longer.
- Yields 8 servings.

ACKNOWLEDGMENTS

To my patient husband, Dave, and our three wonderful children.

ABOUT THE AUTHOR

Josie Riviera is a USA TODAY bestselling author of contemporary, inspirational, and historical sweet romances that read like Hallmark movies. She lives in the Charlotte, NC, area with her wonderfully supportive husband. They share their home with an adorable shih tzu, who constantly needs grooming, and live in an old house forever needing renovations.

To receive my Newsletter and your free sweet romance novella ebook as a thank you gift, sign up HERE.

Become a member of my Read and Review VIP Facebook group for exclusive giveaways and ARCs.

josieriviera1@gmail.com
josieriviera.com

ALSO BY JOSIE RIVIERA

Seeking Patience

Seeking Catherine (always Free!)

Seeking Fortune

Seeking Charity

Seeking Rachel

The Seeking Series

Oh Danny Boy

I Love You More

A Snowy White Christmas

A Portuguese Christmas

Holiday Hearts Book Bundle Volume One

Holiday Hearts Book Bundle Volume Two

Holiday Hearts Book Bundle Volume Three

Holiday Hearts Volume Four

Candleglow and Mistletoe

Maeve (Perfect Match)

A Christmas To Cherish

A Love Song To Cherish

A Valentine To Cherish

A Christmas Puppy To Cherish

A Homecoming To Cherish

Romance Stories To Cherish

Aloha to Love

Sweet Peppermint Kisses

Valentine Hearts Boxed Set

1-800-CUPID

1-800-CHRISTMAS

1-800-IRELAND

1-800-SUMMER

The 1-800-Series Sweet Contemporary Romance Bundle

Irish Hearts Sweet Romance Bundle

Holly's Gift

A Chocolate-Box Valentine

A Chocolate-Box Christmas

A Chocolate-Box New Years

A Chocolate-Box Summer Breeze

A Chocolate-Box Christmas Wish

A Chocolate-Box Irish Wedding

Chocolate-Box Hearts

Chocolate-Box Hearts Volume Two

Recipes from the Heart

Leading Hearts

All books are FREE on Kindle Unlimited.

A CHRISTMAS TO CHERISH (A SWEET CHRISTIAN ROMANCE) PREVIEW

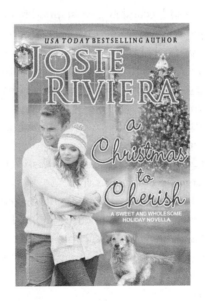

CHAPTER ONE

Emmanuelle Sumter surveyed the picturesque town of Cherish, South Carolina, brightly lit in crimson and green holiday decor. The town looked as if it had emerged from a

Christmas card. Glittering frost framed bare tree branches, and local artists were setting up their canvases for an art walk. The coldness in the air was soundless and serene, comforting in its own way.

She exited the Cherish Central train station, zippered her cobalt-blue puffer coat to her chin, and stepped onto the curb.

Who believed an actual, breathing town could resemble a holiday snow globe?

Evidently, her friend Dorothy did, considering her enthusiasm whenever she described her idyllic South Carolina town.

Emmanuelle stood on the curb and shoved her hands in her pockets. A cold December gust slapped her cheeks, sharp streams of frigid air. She swept a wisp of hair from her cheek and searched for Nicholas, Dorothy's older brother. He was supposed to pick her up. People were shouting greetings, kissing, cooing over babies. A teeming mass of humanity.

But no Nicholas.

A taxi's horn spiked. Emmanuelle jumped, an involuntary nervous reaction.

Take a deep breath. Relax. Dorothy had assured her Cherish was a safe haven, a harbor in a storm.

Repeating her mantra, Emmanuelle hailed the black-bearded taxi driver parked at the curb. She still didn't see any sign of Nicholas, so she'd take the cab.

She handed the driver her suitcase, then slid into the backseat and gave the address of Dorothy's music store, Musically Yours.

They passed charming shops decorated in glittering lights, and a sign advertising a historic home tour. A few minutes later, the driver pointed at the Musically Yours lighted outdoor sign and idled at the corner of Myrtle and Magnolia Streets.

"The store's two hoots and a holler away, ma'am." He hoisted her suitcase from the trunk and set it on the sidewalk. "We've reached your destination."

Destination. Was this where her journey ended after a year filled with pain and abuse? Did hope and encouragement wait for her in this little town?

A new life. With perseverance, she could start fresh.

"Thanks." She climbed from the taxi, paid the driver and grabbed her suitcase.

Daylight faded as dusk crept in, and she tipped her head to take in Evergreen Street. Family-owned businesses had switched on their storefront lights, transforming the town into a fairy-tale sparkle of miniature white lights. The tantalizing scent of honey roasted almonds wafted through the air. Boughs of fragrant holly tied with red velvet bows hung cheerily from tall solitary lampposts. Bright-faced children skipped by, lifting their faces skyward to catch a sprinkling of snow. Their conscientious parents followed close behind.

"Emmanuelle! You arrived right on time!" Dorothy flung open the door of the music store and pressed a welcoming kiss to Emmanuelle's cheek. Dorothy's brown hair was swept up in a French braid, her creamy complexion glowing with an enthusiasm Emmanuelle didn't recall from their days working as struggling musicians in New York.

Dorothy had lived there before moving back to Cherish, her hometown, and marrying her high school crush, Ryan Edwards. He had been an opera star in the making and had given up his touring career to settle in Cherish. They were newlyweds. They were in love.

Love. The beginning was always so alluring. It was the end Emmanuelle feared.

Dorothy regarded the departing taxi. "Apparently Nicholas didn't pick you up?"

"I didn't see him so I took a cab."

Emmanuelle turned from Dorothy and admired Musically Yours' frosty window display, bedecked in an infinite array of treble clef signs. A pine wreath, embellished in antique ornaments—tiny pianos, violins, and harps—adorned the front door.

"It's wonderful," she said. "You've worked so hard to set this up."

"Thanks. Ryan and I are still learning the business, and we're inspired by anything musical."

Emmanuelle smiled, but then shivered. "It's colder here than I expected. At least the blizzard that threatened to shut down New York never came."

"The storm hit after you left," Dorothy replied. "You escaped the worst of it."

Did she? She couldn't answer at first, finally whispering, "Hopefully."

Dorothy raised a delicate eyebrow, but Emmanuelle didn't elaborate. Sure, she'd escaped the snowstorm. An escape from George, her ex, was yet to be determined.

Please God, be with me now in my dark season, when I'm so out of place. The world around me is glowing with the promise of Christmas and I feel dark and empty inside.

She leaned forward to admire two animated polar bears sitting amidst the treble clef signs in the shop's window. Beneath a starry sky, the bears tapped drums to the tune of "Jingle Bells."

"Very clever." She couldn't help a grin. "Thanks for the invite to Cherish."

"We're thrilled you agreed to join us for Christmas." Dorothy grabbed her hands for a reassuring squeeze. She was so pleasant and gracious, Emmanuelle thought. So jovial.

On the other hand, Emmanuelle felt the opposite. All she had become in twenty-five years—a dependable, straightforward woman as well as an esteemed harpist—she'd lost in six months to George.

She'd once been like Dorothy, resilient, independent and a woman of God.

Her ex had taken it all away.

Deep in her coat pocket, her fingers worried an angel ornament she'd purchased at the New York airport. For her, the ornament symbolized the sacred Christmas season, its optimism, dreams, and promise.

She hadn't taken it out of her pocket yet.

"You've been difficult to reach these past few months." Dorothy studiously appraised Emmanuelle. "You hardly ever answered your phone."

"I've been busy with concert engagements." Emmanuelle forced her features to remain blank. "You know, musician stuff." It was a lie, and with the lie came heaviness, a wide band of disapproval. Where had her sense of decency gone?

She tightened her paisley scarf around her neck. Although the violent purple and yellow bruises had faded, she still felt self-conscious.

Dorothy guided her into the music store. "My brother will blame his forgetfulness on his new job, or that gigantic puppy he bought at the animal shelter. You'd think he'd know better at thirty years old."

"He's a good guy," Emmanuelle said. "Nicholas and I Skyped every night for months when you were in rehab."

"Thanks to you both, I'm better." Dorothy smiled. "And most important, thanks to God."

Once, Emmanuelle would have readily agreed. God was her salvation, her refuge. Now she didn't know how to answer because her faith had wavered.

Truly I tell you, if you have faith as small as a mustard seed, you can say to this mountain, "Move from here to there," and it will move. The verse from Matthew 17-20 came to her mind, a reminder of her strength. All she had to do was reach for it, if she was brave enough.

Inside the store, Dorothy ran a finger along one of the shelves, grinning when she was assured it was dust free. "Ryan and I purchased a cottage-style bungalow four blocks from here and there's an extra bedroom."

"This is your first Christmas as a married couple." Emmanuelle set her suitcase out of the way of a passing customer. "Please celebrate the holiday without me in the middle."

"I insist you stay with us."

"For an entire month?" Emmanuelle shook her head. "Insist all you want. I booked a room at the Cherish Hills Inn. You raved about the inn's accommodations being top-quality when you returned to Cherish for your brother's wedding last year."

"The wedding that didn't happen." Ruefully, Dorothy sighed. "Nicholas is still healing from the embarrassment and heartbreak."

The ending stages of love. Dreams shattered.

Without warning, the front door burst open. Instinctively, Emmanuelle held up a hand, shielding herself from view.

A heavy-set woman, her hair helmeted in a tight gray bun, ambled inside. She called out a jovial hello to Dorothy.

"Be with you in a minute, Mrs. McManus." Dorothy gave a flap of her hands, and then turned back to Emmanuelle. "Sorry. What were we discussing?"

Emmanuelle blew out a breath. This uneasiness, this fear of being followed, had to stop.

Still shaken, she kept her focus on a Mozart statue topped with a red plush Santa hat sitting on the counter.

"We were discussing the wedding that didn't happen," she replied. "Whenever Nicholas and I talked when you were in rehab, he always reminded me we should place our trust in God."

"Sadly, people change, beliefs change." Worry replaced Dorothy's earlier smile. "Hard knocks can shake the faith of the most devout. I pray he'll go to church again because he's faltered since the breakup."

Suggesting Emmanuelle put her suitcase behind the front counter, Dorothy led her past a display table. As Dorothy paused to rearrange two pairs of oboe earrings so they lined up side by side, she said, "God had other plans for him and for me. I believe things work out for the best."

Emmanuelle frowned and nodded, aborting both actions.

For Dorothy, perhaps. For Ryan. For anyone in this idyllic snow globe town. But not for me. And apparently not for Nicholas.

Her cell phone buzzed. She retrieved it from her tote bag and scanned the screen. *Unknown caller.* Her heart stopped. A telemarketer? A wrong number?

"Who is it?"

Looking up, she saw Dorothy was studying her with keen interest.

"No one." Fumbling, Emmanuelle tucked the phone back into her faux leather tote. "You're right. People change for many reasons." And she'd changed most of all. She'd been a competent, successful woman. Now a chill crept up her spine when a door opened into a harmless music store.

"Are you okay?" Dorothy asked.

"I'm fine, just tired from traveling." Emmanuelle's eyes welled with tears, and she averted her gaze. She'd applied makeup, the first time in months, attempting to conceal her sleep deprivation. The endless worrying and crying had taken a toll.

"We're organizing a concert in the town square the weekend before Christmas," Dorothy was saying. "I meant to ask you to bring your harp—"

"My harp weighs nearly eighty pounds." She picked up a pair of piano earrings and fingered the tiny keyboard. "It's in New York."

Broken. She wouldn't reveal how George had destroyed her harp in one of his lightning-fast rages. The memory caused a block of ice to form in her stomach, a block that she knew would be slow to thaw. She hated the thought of her beloved instrument, splintered into pieces, lying on a New York curb under a pile of snow.

Better the harp than you splintered into pieces.

But his shouted insults and rough slaps had been her fault. She'd provoked him.

No, no, no. Her inner voice took on a sharp edge. That was the old Emmanuelle talking. The new Emmanuelle knew she wasn't a dishtowel to be thrown around on a whim. In hindsight, she should have known George was abusive. The warning signs were there.

She blew out a breath. She'd resolved to find peace and comfort in this holiday ... in this town ... somewhere ... and find her footing again.

"Enough about me." She set down the earrings and dismissed herself with a flutter of her fingers. "Where's Ryan?"

"He's rehearsing in nearby Stanley Valley today and will arrive this evening. He'll be singing 'O Holy Night' for a Christmas Cantata service. He gives so freely of his talent." Dorothy's smile was as radiant as a Merry Christmas bouquet. "He's featured throughout the Carolinas in many guest appearances. Plus, the Atlanta opera house asked him to perform the role of Zoroastro in Handel's opera, *Orlando.* I'm incredibly proud of him."

"You should be." Dorothy's smile was contagious, and Emmanuelle managed a warm grin. "He's famous and extremely talented."

"And you? Any upcoming concerts?"

"None." She answered in a firm tone that she expected would discourage her friend from probing. Judging by the way Dorothy's eyebrows drew together, she'd succeeded.

Fortunately, an acoustic guitar arrangement of "Lo, How a Rose Is Blooming" piped in the background, the ideal holiday music to smooth a lull in the conversation.

"I'm sure you're keen to check in." Dorothy broke the silence. "I'll deal with these last few customers, close the store, and give you a lift. Unless you'd rather walk the three blocks to the inn?"

"No, no. I'll wait for you."

She'd never walk alone again. Not in New York, not in Cherish. Not anywhere, because she'd never feel safe again.

Dorothy gestured toward the front of the store. "If you care to browse, the Christmas music section is on your left. There's a lovely harp arrangement of *The Nutcracker*."

"Thanks. Your store is a music-lover's dream."

Intrigued, Emmanuelle stepped past a buyer laden with music bookmarks and made her way to the sheet music. She thumbed through endless arrangements of Christmas solos, wondering what madness had brought her to this town. She didn't belong here among all this gaiety. Her sadness was a burden refusing to go away.

Disheartened, she stared, trancelike, at the display window. A whimsical model train circled the polar bears, and the sight was enchanting.

Beyond, past the cheery town, past the exuberant children and the enormous Christmas tree illuminating the town square, a darkened sky had followed dusk.

*** End of Excerpt *A Christmas To Cherish* by Josie Riviera ***

Want more contemporary inspirational romances? Continue reading:

A Christmas To Cherish
A Valentine To Cherish
A Christmas Puppy To Cherish
and my 3 book bundle:
Romance Stories To Cherish

All FREE on Kindle Unlimited!

Made in the USA
Middletown, DE
05 May 2022

65356013R00056